D0402862

What's Bugging You?

Workbook & Journal

What's Bugging You? Workbook & Journal
Copyright © 2010 by Keith Harrell.
All rights reserved. Printed in the United States of America.
No part of this book may be used or reproduced in any manner
whatsoever without written permission, except in the case of brief
quotations embodied in critical articles and reviews.
For information, contact Harrell Performance Systems, Inc.,
8374 Market Street, #504, Lakewood Ranch, FL 34202
or visit our website www.superfantastic.com

Designed by mudpie graphics, inc.
Illustrations by Walt Floyd

Library of Congress Cataloging-in-Publication Data
has been applied for.

ISBN 978-0-9826101-1-4

"You're Either On the Way, or In the Way"

What's Bugging You?

Workbook & Journal

How to **Motivate Yourself** and Others Through Teamwork, Change, and Attitude!

Keith Harrell

An imprint of HPS Publishers

Foreword

When Keith asked me to work on this project with him, I was not expecting to have my life transformed. A lover of the written word, I have kept diaries since I was old enough to write a complete thought. As a child, I'd record my dreams, goals, and unspoken feelings. The process has carried over into adulthood, except now it's called journaling. I have found journaling to be a liberating path to self-discovery—a safe, creative place where I can think outside of the box, unburden myself, dream, and "rest on the page."

So, as I focused on my contribution to the *Workbook & Journal*, and reread the *What's Bugging You?* book, I found myself becoming more introspective as I pondered the question, *"What's Bugging You?"* Anxiety surrounding unresolved childhood issues surfaced in my daily journal. The need to have a long overdue talk with my father took on an unsettling urgency. I realized that I could no longer put it off. The only problem was, he'd died more than 14 years ago; and though his gravesite was in a nearby city, I could not recall the name of the cemetery, nor how to get there since I'd not returned to the site since his burial. An Internet search early one Sunday morning put me in contact with a kindhearted woman who, after several unsuccessful attempts, located the cemetery where my father's cremains are buried. Then fear kicked in, and I found myself procrastinating and making excuses, trying to convince myself that going to the gravesite was irrational and unnecessary. I decided to let it go . . . at least momentarily. The following day, while on my way to the grocery store, I found myself on the freeway heading toward the cemetery. By the time I pulled into the parking lot, I knew I had to locate my father's plot and finally speak what had been left unsaid for too long.

As I sat at his gravesite, I spoke from my heart and had the tearful breakdown and emotional breakthrough that I'd been wanting, but hadn't known how to achieve. Giving myself permission to fully explore what had been bugging me for so long allowed me to get to the root of the issue and achieve closure. My spirit feels lighter now. I can honestly say that my attitude is better.

As you embark upon this 40-day course, I hope you also have a life-changing breakthrough. The daily act of journaling, writing one's thoughts and feelings in longhand, clarifies thought, unleashes pent up emotions, and can lead to positive changes in attitude, circumstances, and overall well being.

Arabella Grayson, January 2010

When we are no longer able to change a situation,
we are challenged to change ourselves.

VIKTOR E. FRANKL

How to Use This Workbook and Journal

This book is designed to help you identify those life challenges that continue to bug you. By reading the stories, doing the simple exercises in this workbook and journaling daily, you will examine the patterns in your behavior and attitude that get in your way, and change them to enhance your personal and professional success.

Why the 40-day format? Since the beginning of time, the number forty has been associated with a period of renewal and transformation. Today, we have come to regard the 40-day cycle with a period of "testing and trial" that ends with the hope of "restoration, revival, and renewal."

Studies also show that it takes 21 days to form a habit. It stands to reason, if you are willing to earnestly apply the seven Guiding Principle Steps (GPS) and Be-Attitudes contained in this workbook over the next 40 days, that you can expect a personal transformation in your attitude and behavior. Expect to go through a range of emotions throughout the course of this journey. Change isn't always easy, but it is constant and necessary because it produces the power for growth.

Based on the book by the same title, *What's Bugging You?*, this workbook continues with the adventures of Chris, a distraught business executive who is on his way to corporate headquarters when an unexpected encounter with an ant scientist leads him down a path of self-discovery, and newfound personal and professional success.

Chris learns how the highly developed work ethic and behaviors of God's tiniest creatures make them masters of *teamwork*, *change*, and *attitude*. Through practicing the Guiding Principle Steps and Be-Attitudes, Chris is able to make the distinction between AINTS and A.N.T.S. (**A**ttitudes **N**avigating **T**oward **S**uccess) and adopt a winning attitude.

You'll dive deeper into the lives of the aints (those ants who are struggling with numerous attitude problems) featured in the book. And you'll be introduced to a few new ones. Either way, you'll begin to see some of the same characteristics on your team and in your organization, and maybe even in yourself. But you'll also receive the help you need to transform those negative characteristics into the attitudes, behaviors, and performances needed to succeed.

Over the next 40 days, commit to do the work: read the stories, complete all of the exercises, respond in writing to the questions, and write your journal entries each day.

Write about whatever's on your mind and use additional sheets of paper as needed. Set aside enough time each day to complete the exercises in an unrushed manner, without distractions and interruptions. This is your time for self-discovery and a guaranteed attitude tune-up.

Why Use Ants
to Illustrate Attitude?

Because when it comes to having a work ethic, these tiny creatures are by far one of the wisest, most organized, and industrious teams on the planet:

The ant is self-governing. It needs no prompting to act. Highly self-motivated and disciplined, the ant takes the initiative to do whatever is needed to get the job done. High standards are the only acceptable measure of success. These self-sacrificing creatures work effectively and efficiently, knowing that their success secures the future of the colony. Without fear of policy or threat of termination the ant is driven to excel.

The hardworking ants plan for the future—seasonally storing and gathering provisions and food regardless of adverse weather or other challenges that arise. Nothing stops their work. For this reason, during harvest time they are able to feast on the fruits of their labor.

Highly organized, the ants work with purpose and intention. They know their jobs and stick to them.

However, when emergencies arise, the ant shifts its focus, pitching in when and where needed with a can-do attitude. Determined, focused, and goal oriented, the ant is unstoppable in its pursuits. Ants continue on no matter the circumstances. They always do what needs to be done to complete the task.

We can all learn life-changing behaviors from our friends, the ants.

Remember, your past may have impacted your present, but it does not dictate your future. You are predestined for greatness, because *teamwork*, *change*, and a *winning attitude* . . . live within you!

Effort only fully releases its reward
after a person refuses to quit.

NAPOLEAN HILL

Contract

I, _____, believe in the power of attitude to change my personal circumstance and am willing to undergo a guided 40-day exploration of those areas that are undermining my own success. I, _____, understand that this process may bring up issues and emotions that I will have to deal with in order to discard negative habits and to allow positive change in my life. During this 40-day period, I commit to being my own best friend by treating myself with kindness and compassion—keeping an open mind and heart—and not beating myself up for attitudes and behaviors that I find less than appealing in myself during the course of this self-examination. I, _____, am committing to adequate rest, healthy eating, daily exercise (20-minute walks count), and self-nurturing for the duration of the process.

_____

(Signature)

_____

(Start Date)

_____

(Completion Date—40 Days from Start Date)

You can't control what bugs you, but you can control how you respond to it.

The *What's Bugging You? Workbook & Journal* is based on the book by the same title. The simple parable is about a working professional whose life has been turned upside down. His wife is contemplating ending their 21-year marriage. The recent downturn in the economy has almost wiped out his 401k. His mortgage is in foreclosure. His health is being challenged by high blood pressure, high cholesterol, and a tremendous amount of stress. In addition, rumor has it that his company is on the verge of a major downsize.

Your situation may or may not seem as complicated or overwhelming as Chris's, the subject of the book, but no matter what your circumstance, I'm sure there's something bugging you. The fact that you're reading this now lets me know this.

If you were to honestly answer the question *"What's Bugging You?,"* how long would your list be? It seems as though something is always bugging people nowadays. Whether it's the economy, your marriage, your finances, your health, your job, a teammate, or even something as uncontrollable as the weather, the list of things that bug you can be endless.

Doing the exercises in this workbook and journal will help you identify *What's Bugging You?* and to determine whether it is deeply rooted in your heart. Over the next 40 days, as you complete the reading and exercises, you will discover a course of action to remove the *"I"* in aints and move to the rank of A.N.T.S. (**A**ttitudes **N**avigating **T**oward **S**uccess).

What's Bugging You?
Write a very brief description of three things that frustrate you.

_____ 1. _____

_____

_____

_____ 2. _____

_____

_____

_____ 3. _____

_____

_____

What's Bugging Your Team?
Briefly describe three everyday things that frustrate your team.

_____ 1. _____

_____

_____

_____ 2. _____

_____

_____

_____ 3. _____

_____

_____

Now go back and look at *What's Bugging You?* and what's bugging your team. To the left of each number, rank them on a scale of 1 to 10 (10 being the highest) according to what degree the particular situation is bugging you. Anything above a 7 is most likely rooted in your heart and may be infecting your attitude, behavior, and performance and has now become an aint, which you'll need to name (I'll explain this concept in more detail later).

_____

_____

_____

_____

To reveal myself openly and honestly
takes the rawest kind of courage.

JOHN POWELL

One of the most powerful words in the English language is *attitude*, because attitude—whether good or bad—is involved in everything you do, say, and believe. Attitude is a choice, and you are the only one who decides what kind of attitude you will wear on any given day. To illustrate the power of attitude, take the following assessment.

Rate Your Attitude

Circle the number that best represents your response to each statement. When you've finished, total the scores for each column and then add the column totals for your final score.

	Almost Always	Sometimes	Never
1. I recognize opportunities in new situations.	5	3	1
2. I am doubtful of new situations until they've been proven.	1	3	5
3. I believe there's nothing better for me at this time.	1	3	5

	Almost Always	*Sometimes*	*Never*
4. I am concerned about others' fear of change.	1	3	5
5. I know I'll do well in a new situation.	5	3	1
6. I trust those responsible for implementing change.	5	3	1
7. I anticipate the good that comes with each new day.	5	3	1
8. I feel like things are too good to be true, and will soon change.	1	3	5
9. I doubt that I can complete what needs to be done today.	1	3	5
10. I am confident the things that need to get done today will get done— and done well.	5	3	1
11. I feel I'm going through the motions and wish something would happen to change things.	1	3	5
12. I hope my job lasts and my boss thinks my work is okay.	1	3	5
13. I look forward to discovering new opportunities daily.	5	3	1
14. I feel my boss would say I have a positive attitude.	5	3	1
15. I don't let minor things upset me.	5	3	1
16. I feel enthusiastic about my life and job.	5	3	1

	Almost Always	Sometimes	Never
17. I believe my team would say I have a good attitude.	5	3	1
18. I feel I have a positive attitude.	5	3	1
19. I usually treat others with compassion and patience.	5	3	1
20. I have had a high level of creativity for the last several weeks.	5	3	1

COLUMN TOTALS: _____ +_____ +_____

GRAND TOTAL: _____

A score of 90–100 equals a consistently positive, proactive approach to life's challenges and opportunities.

A score of 70–89 equals an attitude reflective of experiencing the ups and downs of "good days and bad days."

A score of 50–69 equals a tendency to focus on the negative—the glass being half empty, instead of half full.

A score of 0–49 equals pervasive negative thoughts and feelings that are holding you back.

What did the assessment reveal about your attitude?

_____

_____

_____

_____

_Attitude: The good news is you don't have to buy it,
but you do have to develop it._

The exercises in this workbook are based on seven *Guiding Principle Steps* and *Be-Attitudes* that constitute ethical behavior. When learned and practiced, they will put you in the mindset to take actions that result in positive outcomes.

Why Guiding Principle Steps (GPS)?

Having principles as a foundation in life or in business will not only provide a solid foundation to stand on, but to navigate through, around, under, or over whatever you're facing.

Most of us are familiar with the mobile GPS devices that are now available in newer automobiles. GPS stands for Global Positioning System, a technology that can determine the location of a car, and will voice-navigate it to coordinates input on a keyboard; calculating the quickest route to your desired destination. If you by chance take a wrong turn and get off course, the GPS device recalculates to help you navigate to your destination. No matter how many times you get lost or don't follow directions, it will always recalculate—providing you with new route information to get you to your final destination.

The GPS (Guiding Principle Steps) operate in similar fashion. They are the coordinates that will enable you to stand on a principle, and keep you on course as you navigate, and take the appropriate steps and actions needed to make it to your intended destination.

Seven Guiding Principle Steps

Teamwork—Live the Vision

Accountability—Say No to the Blame Game

Ethical Execution—Do What's Right Because It's Right

Embrace Change—Convert Turning Points to Learning Points

Commit to Win—Do More Than is Expected

Awareness—Notice What's Needed and Do What's Necessary

Attitude is Everything—If Something Is Wrong, Make It Right

Take a lesson from the ants,
learn from their ways and be wise!

PROVERBS 6:6

Identify three guiding principles from the previous page:

1. _____

_____

2. _____

_____

3. _____

_____

Example: Accountability—Say No to the Blame Game

Why are these principles important to you?

_____

_____

_____

_____

_____

_____

_____

_____

_____

_____

How might incorporating the Guiding Principle Steps into your life improve your situation?

_____

_____

_____

_____

_____

_____

_____

_____

_____

_____

_____

_____

_____

_____

All that a man achieves and all that he fails to achieve
is the direct result of his own thoughts.

JAMES ALLEN

What are the Be-Attitudes?

The Be-Attitudes are a "right now" mindset that, when modeled, enable an individual, team, or organization to improve their overall performance and success.

To eliminate bad attitudes adopt the Be-Attitudes and become as wise and industrious as the ants:

- *Be supportive* of the team
- Strive to *be accountable*
- *Be a change embracer*
- Adopt an attitude to *be coachable*
- Always *be performance- and integrity-driven*
- *Be responsible*
- Work with an attitude to *be the difference*

Why the Be-Attitudes?

The Be-Attitudes help us prepare a "right now" mindset to take action. Taking the right steps to find your way through an ineffective mindset will move you into the ranks of the A.N.T.S. (**A**ttitudes **N**avigating **T**oward **S**uccess). The final critical piece is not just what we do, the steps we take, and the principles that we stand on, but it's our attitude and *how we do it.*

Review the Be-Attitudes listed below. Then create several additional Be-Attitudes that you can adopt to give yourself a "right now" mindset.

Add to the Be-Attitude list below:

Be Supportive	Be-_____
Be Accountable	Be-_____
Be a Change Embracer	Be-_____
Be Coachable	Be-_____
Be Performance- and Integrity-Driven	Be-_____
Be Responsible	Be-_____
Be the Difference	Be-_____

_____

_____

_____

_____

_____

_____

_____

_____

_____

_____

_____

_____

_____

_____

_____

_____

_____

_____

_____

_____

_____

_____

_____

_____

Whether you think you can or think you can't, you're right.

HENRY FORD

Here are four additional stories that support those in the book *What's Bugging You?*, a parable I wrote to illustrate unique insights about attitude and behavior and how they affect performance and impact our relationships, even when we're not conscious of what we're doing. Based on the Guiding Principle Steps and their corresponding Be-Attitudes, each story highlights a profound truth about teamwork, change, and attitude. Each story introduces a character—What's In It For Me, Pretender, Slacker, and Saboteur—whose ineffective attitude bugs his co-workers, causing far-reaching disorganization and devastating morale issues within the organization, and jeopardizing the very existence of the entire colony.

Chris, an IT sales manager, is enroute to corporate headquarters to meet with the vice president of Human Resources to explain his team's downturn in sales and the sinking morale within his division. Sparked by a conversation with Herman, an enthusiastic ant scientist and fellow passenger, Chris falls asleep inflight and dreams he is the manager of Human Resources at an ant colony. Charged with terminating the aints (good ants gone bad) who are causing trouble within the ranks and jeopardizing the very existence of the entire colony, Chris is inspired to change his attitude and make his division a winning team.

After you've read each story, write down what comes to mind and complete the companion exercises following each Profile. You might be surprised to discover one of your own limiting attitudes.

Code Name:
WIIFM (What's In It For Me)
Aint Doing That Job

WIIFM has a What's In It For Me attitude. Always looking out for Number One, he tends to believe the world owes him, that he is entitled to his desires . . . usually at someone else's expense.

The Guiding Principle Step (GPS):
Commit to Win—Do More Than is Expected
and the Be-Attitude: *Be Coachable*

It was after lunch when Chris spotted the Food Gathering Division director who had been trying to get in to see him before the latest commotion, and he was glad to run into him between meetings. His area had been hit hard by the recent events. Food shortages, the engineering crisis, and a tough work environment had the colony in a crisis: missed deadlines, unfinished projects, and morale at an all-time low.

"Hey Stan, I've been meaning to get back to you—"

"Hi there, Chris . . . no problem."

Chris nodded. "What can I do for you?"

Stan Susten-ant took a deep breath. "Well, I've been wanting to talk to you about Terry WIIFM (What's In It For Me). Things have been escalating since we last discussed his situation, and yesterday it all started again. His mother called while I was in a meeting and left quite a message."

Chris's eyes widened. "Again? What does she want now?"

"What do you think? Seems she heard about her son's write-up after his latest blunder in the field with the scouting expedition. You do remember that she was the reason he was promoted so quickly—obviously too quickly.

"She is convinced that the real problem is that his supervisor and co-workers aren't supporting him. She said she wants him transferred and she has some 'ideas' she wants to come and discuss with me regarding—and I quote—'future plans and placement opportunities for her son.' She won't talk to his manager—she insists on meeting with me.

"Chris, I have no clue how to handle this. Since when do parents call and want to review every management decision like their kid is still in *school?* I've never seen anything like it, and I understand the other ants in the department are getting pretty fed up with the special treatment. They've had to climb the ladder just like everyone else before them, yet he's barely out of school and expecting to enjoy the perks of the senior ants."

Stan went on, "You know, we have several managers who are also struggling with issues like Terry WIIFM's. It seems like the younger generation is an entirely different breed—many of them don't show up for work on time and frequently expect promotions before they're ready, and big salaries before they've earned them. One of their favorite responses when you ask them to do something they don't want to do is, *'Why me?'* A couple of weeks ago, I had one manager telling me that his new hire hadn't worked a full week before she was asking if she could have an advance for an upcoming vacation!"

Chris rolled his eyes. "Yeah, what's missing here is an understanding of the Guiding Principle Step: *Commit To Win—Do More Than Is Expected.*

"Our accelerated culture doesn't help much—they're moving faster than we ever did, with access to whatever they want in seconds on their electronic devices. Quite a few of these younger ants have grown up in homes with a sense of entitlement and immediate gratification. They've never had to wait for anything, or learn how to hang in there when things get tough. A lot of them are probably smarter sooner than most of us were at that age—the only problem is that knowledge is only part of the equation. As we both know, there are some things that only come with time."

"Yeah . . . like *experience,*" Stan broke in. "And wisdom. And patience. Then there's judgment that's been tested by time and trials. And what about plain old *respect*?"

"I know, I know . . . it's frustrating to say the least. Doting parents often come with the package, and it can be a pretty tough combination to work with. But Terry WIIFM *does* have a lot of potential, and we don't want to lose him to another colony—we just want to slow him down a bit and help him get the right foundation in place so that he'll have a solid career here. I like him, and he does have the desire to learn. I think the key for us when working with the younger generation is learning how to coach them, versus trying to manage them. So for now let's set up a meeting with Terry WIIFM's manager—without his parents— and see what we can work out."

They arrived at Chris's office, where his assistant was waiting with several phone messages.

Stan was still aggravated, but seemed slightly calmer, since he suspected Chris was right. Times were changing, and even though some things—like character and values—would never change, his division could probably work a little harder to help get the youngsters established and on the right track. They would just have to find a way to help Terry WIIFM understand that he had to cut the apron strings and grow up if he was hoping to get the respect he wanted from his teammates.

Stan agreed to set up a meeting as soon as possible through Barbara, his assist-ant. As Barbara reached for her calendar, a large, angry ant came storming around the corner, talking loudly on her cell phone, pushing a smaller ant out of the way. She snapped a goodbye into the receiver and shoved the phone into her purse as she walked up, all the while eyeing Chris, Stan, and Barbara.

"Is Chris in?" she asked icily. Stan recognized her voice immediately and responded, "Ah, you must be Helicopter Hannah, Terry WIIFM's mother."

"So *you're* Stan. Hmmm." She scanned him and sniffed slightly, making sure he knew that he did not measure up to *her* standards.

Chris spoke up. "What can we do for you, Hannah?"

"I got tired of waiting for a return phone call," she said, whipping a glance toward Stan, "so I decided to stop by and talk with you about my son and the fact that he and his crew"—she waved a jewelry-laden leg at the director—"are clearly mismanaging him. My boy is sensitive, an overachiever who would do much better with the right atmosphere and co-workers. *You're* the HR Director. I think *you* should place him where he will thrive, rather than somewhere he is exploited and abused by the other ants. Recent events have been quite traumatic for him, and he needs a change."

Chris was both annoyed and amused by the pushiness of this hovering parent. He explained calmly to her that they had just been discussing Terry WIIFM when she walked up, and that there were plans to meet with him and work through his latest adjustment issues.

"Great. When should I be here?" she asked.

Stan spoke up. "Actually, we plan to work this out with Terry WIIFM. We've got some good ideas and he'll do fine with his manager's guidance."

"What? I'm his mother, and I need to be at the meeting." Hannah looked surprised.

Chris knew Stan needed some backup. "Hannah, I appreciate your desire to be a good parent. But there are rites of passage that have to be observed in each of our lives. Terry WIIFM is no longer a school child, and you're not doing him any favors treating him like one. Don't you want him to earn the respect of his department? He can't do that until you let him take the next steps as an adult . . . and take them on his own."

Hannah didn't like what she was hearing and bristled as she moved toward both of them. "What I *don't* want is to have either of us pushed around by his peers and managers. You don't know him like I do. A mother always knows what is best for her own son, and I'm only trying to make sure he gets into the right department and has the best possible chances to succeed. If you won't let me attend that meeting, then I'll make this simple. I will pull him out of here and take him somewhere where his talent and skills are more appreciated."

Chris spoke quietly but firmly. "You don't want to threaten anyone, Hannah. We're trying to give him a second chance, which many would say is more than he deserves. He has caused some major delays, and if I recall, it was *you* who insisted on the promotion that put him in a position he was not ready to handle."

Chris' pointed words were all it took to put her over the top. She went into a trembling, red-faced rant for several minutes over the injustices of her son's situation and the incompetence of management before finally grabbing her purse and announcing that her son would be resigning. Immediately.

As she stalked off, Chris turned to Stan and shrugged. "I don't think Hannah knows how much we want the best for Terry WIIFM. Now I understand why he's oblivious to the Be-Attitude—*Be Coachable.* This will be a must in working with our younger generation . . . *and their parents!*"

Later that day, Terry WIIFM walked into Stan's office looking uncomfortable. Embarrassed by his mother's behavior, he launched into an apology.

"I think it's time for me to stand on my own two feet. I'd like to thank you for the opportunities you have already given me and to apologize for not taking advantage of them. I'm not here to resign, I'm here to step up! I'm willing to do whatever it takes to earn the respect and learn the skills needed to be part of this team."

Stan stood and shook Terry WIIFM's hand. "I appreciate you coming in. Let's meet on Monday to put together an action plan that will help us both improve things around here and get this department moving in the right direction. I'll email Chris in HR and update him. I know he'll be excited to hear the news."

As Terry WIIFM turned to walk out, Stan smiled and said, "One more thing . . . I am proud of you."

_____

_____

_____

_____

_____

_____

_____

_____

_____

_____

_____

_____

_____

_____

_____

_____

_____

_____

_____

_____

_____

_____

_____

_____

_____

_____

Tackle the problem, not the person.

Today I . . .

_____

_____

_____

_____

_____

_____

_____

_____

_____

Commit to Win—Do More Than Is Expected

GUIDING PRINCIPLE STEP

_____

_____

_____

_____

_____

_____

_____

_____

_____

_____

_____

_____

_____

_____

_____

_____

_____

_____

_____

_____

_____

Be Coachable

BE-ATTITUDE

Code Name:
WIIFM (What's In It For Me)
Aint Doing That Job

The Aint Profile
General description:
WIIFMs typically have a What's In It For Me attitude. Although they may not have wrong intentions, they tend to be self-centered and have self-serving attitudes—believing that the world owes them something.

WIIFMs often say:
- "This is not the job I was hired for."
- "Why can't I do this job at home? As long as I get it done, why does it matter?"

• "I know I have only been here a couple of months, but I need a vacation."

The Attitude Action
GPS (Guiding Principle Step):
Commit To Win—Do More Than Is Expected

The Be-Attitude: Be Coachable

The Attitude for Success:
The key to success for WIIFMs is getting them to understand that we're all in this together. There's a sacrifice that we all must be willing to make for our individual successes. Guiding them with open and honest two-way communication is critical. Coaching them on how to take proactive action regardless of the sacrifice, as well as staying in a learning mode, are key actions that can help to propel WIIFMs to success.

_____

_____

_____

_____

_____

_____

_____

List the action steps needed to remove the "*I*" from an *Aint Doing That Job* member of your team in order to help him or her move to the ranks of the A.N.T.S. (**A**ttitudes **N**avigating **T**oward **S**uccess):

_____

_____

_____

_____

_____

_____

Are you a WIIFM?

☐ Always ☐ Frequently ☐ Sometimes ☐ Seldom ☐ Never

What impact might this aint have on your performance?

_____

_____

_____

_____

_____

_____

_____

---

*Far and away the best prize that life offers
is the chance to work hard at work worth doing.*

THEODORE ROOSEVELT

Check all statements that apply to you:

☐ I make time to complete my commitments.

☐ I go out of my way to assist others.

☐ I find a need and fill it.

☐ I always do more than is expected of me.

☐ I am considered a dependable person.

☐ My teammates trust me to always do the right thing.

☐ I am considerate of other people's space and property.

☐ I am an attentive listener.

☐ I am grateful.

☐ I have integrity.

☐ People respect my judgment.

☐ I am not judgmental.

☐ I apologize.

☐ I express gratitude for kindnesses, both small and large.

☐ If I am running late, I inform the people who are expecting me.

☐ When I know I am going to miss a deadline, I immediately inform all parties involved.

☐ I keep my word.

☐ I follow through.

☐ I say "thank you."

☐ I arrive late.

☐ I leave early.

☐ I am easily intimidated.

Give recent examples to support three of the statements you checked.

_____

_____

_____

_____

_____

_____

_____

_____

Are you coachable?

Complete the following sentence fragments, choosing what fits your circumstances, and write as much as you need to complete your thoughts.

I think coaches _____

_____

_____

_____

_____

_____

_____

_____

_____

_____

A coach should

_____

_____

_____

_____

_____

_____

_____

_____

_____

The coach decides

_____

_____

_____

_____

_____

_____

_____

_____

_____

_____

I had a coach who

_____

_____

_____

_____

_____

_____

_____

_____

_____

To establish boundaries, a coach

_____

_____

_____

_____

_____

_____

_____

_____

_____

_____

Who are you mentoring or coaching? Why? For what purpose?

_____

_____

_____

_____

_____

_____

_____

_____

_____

_____

_____

_____

_____

_____

_____

One can only face in others what one can face in oneself.

JAMES BALDWIN

During those times when we feel overwhelmed, vulnerable, and stressed by life's many challenges, it's easy to forget our contributions and to fall into "stinking thinking." Self-validation and personal affirmation can provide a needed boost to one's self-esteem and attitude.

Performance Self-Evaluation

Make a complete inventory of those traits and characteristics that have served you well, or that you've always wanted to improve but never took the time, including those childhood traits that you feel you outgrew or skills you never took the time to fully develop. Take your time with this exercise. After you've come up with an exhaustive list, refer to your answers to complete the two exercises that follow.

_____

_____

_____

_____

_____

_____

_____

_____

_____

_____

_____

_____

_____

_____

_____

_____

_____

_____

_____

_____

_____

It is not because things are difficult that we do not dare,
it is because we do not dare that they are difficult.

SENECA

List your strengths:

_____

_____

_____

_____

_____

_____

_____

_____

_____

_____

_____

_____

_____

_____

_____

_____

_____

_____

List those areas that need improvement:

_____

_____

_____

_____

_____

_____

_____

_____

_____

_____

_____

_____

_____

_____

_____

_____

Guard your heart above all else,
for it determines the course of your life.

PROVERBS 4:23

Code Name: Pretender
Aint Ethical

The Pretender is easy to spot: Her scheming, fraudulent ways create uncertainty and confusion. Whether it's pilfering from the lunch room, fudging a bit on the expense report, or telling the little white lie to cover up a minor indiscretion, this lapse in ethics erodes hard earned trust.

The Guiding Principle Step (GPS):
Ethical Execution—Do What's Right Because It's Right
and the Be-Attitude:
Be Performance- and Integrity-Driven

"So *what* happened?

"You told me our department was operating with a budget surplus. Instead, it turns out we're at a 30 percent deficit! Where did the extra money go? I looked like an idiot in that meeting this morning!" Bill roared as Pretender sat at her desk with the spreadsheet open.

"Well, I thought your meeting was next Tuesday. I expected to have more time to go back through the numbers and work everything out, but then you told me yesterday that the meeting was this morning. I kind of panicked. I didn't know what else to do, so I made up some numbers in a second set of books. I wouldn't have done it if things hadn't happened the way they did, but I ran out of time. I'm sorry."

Bill looked at her in disbelief. "Are you kidding me? A second set of books? And tell me, how did you run out of time when you put more hours in here than anyone else I know? You've been working late several nights a week for the past couple of months. What are you doing with your time?"

Pretender fidgeted in her chair. "Well . . . I've been busy and distracted by other things during the day, and a lot of my evening hours have been devoted to a . . . " she hesitated and went slightly pink, " . . . a genealogy project I'm working on for my family so I've needed to use the company computer. I didn't realize how far behind I was in my work until yesterday, and when I saw how much I had to do, it just seemed easier to throw something together and hope no one looked too close until I could fix things." She paused. "I was afraid you would be upset when you saw that I really don't even know where we stand on the budget."

"Yes, you could say I'm upset. But I'm more upset about how you handled the situation than the mistake itself. Don't you realize how important your word is, Pretender? I trusted you. I was operating on the information you were giving me, and now it turns out you were not only sloppy in your work, but you were deliberately unethical in how you handled the problem. How do you possibly justify that kind of behavior when you know that one of our most important Guiding Principle Steps is to *do what's right?*"

"I know, I know . . . but that sounds easier to do than it really is . . . especially under pressure." Pretender leaned back and stared at the ceiling.

Bill sighed. "What happened to you? When I promoted you two years ago, it was because you worked harder than anyone else, and you really cared about doing things with integrity. There were a lot of employees who had stronger marketing backgrounds, but there was no one I trusted more. Doesn't that trust mean anything to you?"

Chris cleared his throat at that moment, and they both looked at him.

"Oh. Sorry, Chris. How long have you been standing there?" Bill looked frustrated and tired. He glanced at his watch. "The time got away from me. We were about halfway through, but now that you're here, let's just deal with it. Do you want to meet in my office?"

Pretender sat up straight as they explained the seriousness of the situation. She got up slowly, and the three of them walked into Bill's nearby office.

Bill walked behind his desk and the other two pulled up chairs and sat down. Unsure of what Bill had already covered, Chris just started at the beginning, from the alarming survey results and growing employee unrest to the tunneling disaster and resulting danger for the colony, and finally the Board's insistence that Chris deal with the aints who were responsible for the colony's downward spiral. He then revealed that Pretender's name had come up in the surveys as an employee who had willfully compromised the colony's success by violating its Guiding Principle Steps and Be-Attitudes.

Chris went on to tell Pretender several of the survey details. She seemed surprised that her co-workers knew about many of her habits. They revealed that she had been forwarding her office calls to her home to make it seem like she was in the office when she wasn't. And some of the account-ants knew that her expense reports contained frequent padding and several outright false line items. She often used her company telephone credit card for personal business, and crossed other lines between personal and work issues—some small, some not so small—skimming off the top and appropriating colony resources for herself even though she knew better. And when asked about it, she would find a way to avoid the truth.

Bill had been so busy and had trusted her enough that he didn't realize how bad the situation was. That is, until this morning, when he discovered in a budget meeting that his department numbers were much different than those from Accounting. As Bill and Chris spoke with her, Pretender still didn't seem to get why it was such a big deal. To her, it was only a problem because she got caught.

Chris asked Pretender why she felt she needed to put on an act to make others think she was working hard when she wasn't. At first, she refused to admit that she had a problem covering things up, but she finally got honest with them.

"I don't know. Sometimes it's just easier to tell a little white lie . . . everybody does it. I guess I liked that everyone thought I was such a hard worker because I always seemed busy and because of my long hours. It got pretty easy to keep up that front . . . until I got careless, of course, and it all came crashing down. But really, it wasn't *that* bad—if I had been more careful, no one would ever have found out; if I had just had a little more time, I could have gotten everything back on track."

"No, Pretender," Chris interrupted her. "You don't have a time problem. You have an ethics problem. Unfortunately, that is much harder to fix. And as for time, you are out of it. Unless you can prove that you, in fact, did not violate the GPS (Guiding Principle Step) *Ethical Execution—Do What's Right Because It's Right*, then I'm afraid there is nothing left to discuss. The Be-Attitude missing here is obvious: *Be performance-and integrity-driven*."

Pretender saw that her attempts at having everyone think she was a model employee had pretty much crumbled, but she still couldn't totally let go. She looked over at Bill.

"Fine . . . but you will give me a good reference, right?"

Bill looked at her blankly as Chris shook his head and got up from his chair. He didn't understand how she could miss the point of the discussion, but he could guess how things would go if she didn't start caring more about what was on the inside—character and integrity—rather than the show she could put on for others. He left them to finish talking as Bill's assist-ant passed him and walked into the office with a phone message.

_____

_____

_____

_____

_____

_____

_____

_____

_____

_____

_____

_____

_____

As a man thinketh in his heart, so is he.

PROVERBS 23:7

Today I . . .

_____

_____

_____

_____

_____

_____

_____

_____

_____

_____

Ethical Execution—Do What's Right Because It's Right

GUIDING PRINCIPLE STEP

_____

_____

_____

_____

_____

_____

_____

_____

_____

_____

_____

_____

_____

_____

_____

_____

_____

_____

Be Performance– and Integrity–Driven

BE-ATTITUDE

Code Name: Pretender
Aint Ethical

The Aint Profile

General description:

Pretenders are people who are often not honest with themselves or others. They feel like their problem is not a problem as long as they don't get caught.

Pretenders often say:
- "The company's so big they'll never miss these office supplies. Everybody does it."
- "I didn't mean to hurt anybody. It wasn't that big of a deal."
- "If I had more time, I could make it all go away."

The Attitude Action
GPS (Guiding Principle Step):
Ethical Execution—Do What's Right Because It's Right

The Be-Attitude: Be Performance- and Integrity-Driven

The Attitude for Success:
The key to success for Pretenders is for them to recognize that integrity starts with honesty. And truth is the foundation for organizational and professional success. They should also remember that there is no growth in a lie, and one can only go so high being unethical. Eventually, they will crash.

_____

_____

_____

_____

_____

_____

_____

_____

_____

_____

_____

_____

List the action steps needed to remove the "*I*" from an *Aint Ethical* team member in order to help him or her move to the ranks of the A.N.T.S. (**A**ttitudes **N**avigating **T**oward **S**uccess):

_____

_____

_____

_____

_____

_____

Are you a Pretender?
☐ Always ☐ Frequently ☐ Sometimes ☐ Seldom ☐ Never

In what ways can you be more honest with yourself? With the most important people in your life?

_____

_____

_____

_____

_____

_____

_____

_____

_____

_____

_____

_____

_____

_____

_____

_____

_____

_____

_____

_____

_____

_____

_____

_____

_____

The truth shall set you free.

JOHN 8:32

Code Name: Slacker
Aint Trying

When help is needed, look elsewhere—Slacker won't have your back. Adept at finding excuses to get out of work, and creating shortcuts that frequently waste valuable time and resources, he is notoriously unreliable.

The Guiding Principle Step (GPS):
Awareness—Notice What's Needed
and Do What's Necessary
and the Be-Attitude: *Be Responsible*

Stan followed Chris into his office and they both sat down. Glancing at the clock on the wall, Chris saw it was almost time for Slacker to arrive. He went over his hastily scribbled notes with Stan regarding Slacker, who had become a regular in his office. Chris constantly had to mediate various issues with his director, his subordinates, and other employees.

File Notes: *Promoted to management position but currently on probation due to work quality and poor employee relations. Have several complaints against him by other department managers and members of his staff on file. Frequently misses project deadlines and food storage quotas. Uses up sick days early in each quarter and takes unauthorized time. Poor time and resource management skills.*

Fifteen minutes went by, and just as Chris was about to have Barbara, his assist-ant, call over to check on him, Slacker showed up.

"You're late," Stan said.

"Yeah, sorry. I let the time get away from me." Slacker sat down and leaned back in his chair a bit. "I didn't get much infor-mation on what the meeting was about. Is everything OK?"

Chris shrugged. "Well, why don't you tell us? How are things going over in your part of the Field Scout Department these days?"

"Same old stuff—nothing new. Why? Is there a problem?"

Chris recounted his meeting with the senior management team, which ended with their demand that operations be cleaned up immediately so the colony crisis would not get any worse.

"Look, I'm going to be honest with you here, Slacker. When

you were placed on probation six months ago, it was made clear that your performance and commitment to your job were unacceptable. You were informed that you would be watched carefully, and that you were expected to take more personal responsibility, while Stan would work with you to get your productivity up to basic standards. Well, the probation time is up and things have not gotten better since our last meeting. You've been written up twice in the last three months for unauthorized absences, and you're *still* behind in the food stockpiling."

Slacker interrupted him. "Now, wait a minute. It's not my fault that the tunneling project fell apart and threw everyone off schedule."

Stan laughed. "Slacker, you've been running behind on your numbers for the past year-and-a-half. That's a weak excuse, trying to use an incident from last week when work avoidance seems like a legitimate management style to you."

Slacker shrugged. "Well, I don't hear any complaints around here, and I think my style works just fine."

Chris shook his head. "The fact is, you set a terrible example for others. You should be mentoring the younger ants, yet you rarely show up to work on time. You generally disappear when there's work to do, and you miss deadlines on important projects. You are one of a handful of ants who have consistently violated colony protocol and rejected the Guiding Principle Steps that we depend on for our very survival. We can't afford to live with your laziness and your unwillingness to carry your share of the daily responsibilities. They weaken the fabric of who we are.

"Slacker, we have to do what we can to salvage the attitudes and performance of the remaining ants, as well as what's left of the colony's good name. I'm sorry, but we've got a full blown crisis on our hands, and we need every ant on board to deal with it. I'm afraid we've given you plenty of time to turn things around. You knew what needed to be done, but you didn't do what was necessary."

Chris knew Slacker would recognize his final statement from the Guiding Principle Step that hung on the wall outside his own office. Slacker had passed that sign a thousand times, just like all the others posted throughout the work areas. The problem was that he was too busy figuring out ways to get out of work, instead of doing the work, which was necessary to keep his job.

"Slacker, remember success starts with *Awareness—Notice What's Needed and Do What's Necessary: Be Responsible.*"

The reward of a thing well done is to have done it.

RALPH WALDO EMERSON

Today I . . .

_____

_____

_____

_____

_____

_____

_____

_____

_____

_____

_____

Awareness—Notice What's Needed and Do What's Necessary

GUIDING PRINCIPLE STEP

Be Responsible

BE-ATTITUDE

Code Name: Slacker
Aint Trying

The Aint Profile

General description:

Slackers are notoriously known for not pulling their own weight. They are often called "lazy" and are skilled at finding shortcuts and excuses to get out of work. Their work rarely stands out.

Slackers often say:
- "I know the deadline is today, but I didn't have time to get to it."
- "There's got to be a shortcut or an easier way to do this."
- "I'm not going to do that right now. I'll wait until later."

The Attitude Action
GPS (Guiding Principle Step):
Awareness—Notice What's Needed and Do What's Necessary

The Be-Attitude: Be Responsible

The Attitude for Success:
The key to success for Slackers is getting them to take responsibility for pulling their own weight. Giving them recognition, when earned, can help to build their self-esteem. Also, helping them to reach for a personal goal that supports an organizational goal can make them feel important and lead to their becoming a true asset to the team.

_____

_____

_____

_____

_____

_____

_____

_____

_____

List the action steps needed to remove the "T" from an *Aint Trying* member of your team in order to help him or her move to the ranks of the A.N.T.S. (**A**ttitudes **N**avigating **T**oward **S**uccess):

_____

_____

_____

_____

_____

_____

_____

Are you a Slacker?
☐ Always ☐ Frequently ☐ Sometimes ☐ Seldom ☐ Never

How does interacting with a Slacker affect your attitude? Explain a specific incident in detail. How did it make you feel? How did you respond? What was the outcome? How would you respond differently if the situation occurred again?

_____

_____

_____

_____

_____

_____

_____

_____

_____

_____

_____

_____

_____

_____

_____

_____

_____

_____

_____

_____

_____

The man who really wants to do something finds a way;
the other man finds an excuse.

E.C. MCKENZIE

Code Name: Saboteur
Aint Nobody Gonna Win

You can count on Saboteur for underhanded interference that undermines progress and cripples the ambitions of anyone or anything that threatens his agenda. The deliberate destruction caused by his actions has an incalculable human and material cost.

The Guiding Principle Step (GPS):
Attitude is Everything—If Something Is Wrong, Make It Right and the Be-Attitude: *Be the Difference*

Acting on his gut instincts, Chris learned that Saboteur, who worked in the Architecture Department, had been the true reason for the tunneling debacle. He had been the one to give Free Agent the second set of blueprints that had caused all the trouble.

Chris went through his notes once more before Saboteur showed up.

• *Transferred from smaller colony two years ago, quietly and without recommendations*

• *Pattern of taking over staff meetings with his own ideas; general unwillingness to work with others or consider others' concepts equally*

• *Some creative contributions in the Architecture Department but tends to sabotage progress when pressure is high*

• *Architecture manager had been documenting some insubordination issues for several months before HR was contacted*

Chris thought he had most of the pieces already in place, but he knew that this meeting would help him put the complete picture together.

Saboteur's supervisor had been trying to discuss several issues with the aint unsuccessfully, so he had suggested that Chris might do better alone. He leaned back in his chair and rubbed his head. Just then, Barbara let him know that Saboteur had arrived.

He took a deep breath before telling her to show him in. Saboteur sat down and they exchanged courtesy greetings, then Chris got to the heart of the matter.

"We are all trying to work through the aftermath of the recent tunneling disaster, Saboteur, and it involved a lot of departments and a lot of employees. Frankly, however, all roads seem to lead back to you. I'm afraid I need to ask you some hard questions."

Saboteur did not look completely surprised, but he shifted in his seat and crossed his top legs. "Fine. What do you want to know?"

"Well, we could start with why you gave a second set of blueprints to Free Agent when you knew he had already been given the official set from the Architecture Department." Chris looked intently at him, as the defiant ant cleared his throat before speaking.

"He wanted to get the job done quicker. He just didn't read the legend right and miscalculated the distance. Those blueprints were perfectly fine and would have worked if he had not been rushing," Saboteur stated smugly.

"That's not what your supervisor told me. He felt that there was reason to believe you had an axe to grind with management, and that you deliberately gave Free Agent bad specs for the tunnel."

Saboteur sat expressionless for a moment, then turned surly as he realized the truth was out.

"Okay, so there *were* some problems with the blueprints. Look, I had to prove a point. I had already submitted plans that were far better than the ones that were chosen for the project, but they were rejected. There's always been a personality conflict between me and my manager. He never wants to hear my ideas. In this case, I really felt it was unfair that he had me work so long on the blueprints just to tell me that after all my effort, he was going to use someone else's plans . . . especially since it turned out to be a new ant who just started with the department. It wasn't right, and I wanted to let him know how it felt to have everyone look at you like you're a failure."

Chris shook his head as the defiant Red Fire ant's words poured out in a cold fury. "No way! Saboteur, are you telling me you were willing to throw our entire colony into chaos and danger over a *personal grudge?*"

The aint glared at him and his voice hardened as he leaned forward. "Well, I guess we're all a little unhappy these days, aren't we? Things like this only seem to matter when they affect everyone else . . . no one asked me how *I* felt when *I* had my plans rejected or how humiliating it was to see a younger ant's blueprints used instead of *mine*. Maybe now some ants will *think* before they do things." He sat back and adjusted his glasses.

Chris was horrified at the aint's display of petty selfishness and his inability to see that when he hurt one ant, he would be hurting them all; or, if he did see it, that he didn't care. "Saboteur, you have violated one of the most important Guiding Principle Steps of this colony, *Attitude is Everything—If Something Is Wrong, Make It Right.*

"Making something right is far more important than being better than someone else at a game or event. Striving to right a wrong is about gaining possession of the *best* that is in us by defeating the *worst* that is in us.

"Your behavior and attitude have displayed that you have missed an opportunity to *be the difference*. By sabotaging the tunneling project, you have created a colony-wide calamity. You have spoiled your own chances at a successful career, but far worse, you have sacrificed the careers and the lives of others as well. Do you have any clue how devastating your actions were?"

Saboteur looked at him and seemed almost proud that his actions had created chaos that was still echoing throughout the colony. "Well, like *I* said, if someone had cared about what *I* thought, then maybe *I* would care more about what others are dealing with now. Sorry that it has caused so much trouble."

Chris recognized Saboteur's attitude problem—wanting to trash the project since he didn't get to participate in it.

"Okay, I think I've heard enough." Chris was trembling slightly but made sure to maintain his composure as he announced the intentions of the senior management team to dismiss the ants who were behind the colony's upheaval.

The aint stood up as a look of shock crossed his face. "Are you serious? I can't just get a transfer? Since when did they start firing workers?"

Chris' eyes darkened, and he replied, "Since ants started breaking the foundational Guiding Principle Steps and Be-Attitudes that hold our colony together. And the one you broke is one of the most important."

Saboteur gave him a sour look, then turned and stormed out of the office.

_____

_____

_____

_____

_____

The axe you grind cuts both ways.

Today I . . .

_____

_____

_____

_____

_____

_____

_____

_____

_____

_____

Attitude is Everything—
If Something Is Wrong, Make It Right

GUIDING PRINCIPLE STEP

Be the Difference

BE-ATTITUDE

Code Name: Saboteur
Aint Nobody Gonna Win

The Aint Profile
General description:

Saboteurs are people who sabotage projects, situations and opportunities. They may be willing to do anything to stop the success of others. Some Saboteurs are conscious of their destructive plans while others, because of fear and other underlying emotions, may act unconsciously. Some Saboteurs may have a personal grudge that results in a selfish agenda.

Saboteurs often say:

- "I don't care about anything or anyone here."
- "What has happened to me is not right, someone is going to pay for this!"
- "Ha! It'll take forever to fix this."

The Attitude Action
GPS (Guiding Principle Step):
Attitude is Everything—If Something Is Wrong, Make It Right

The Be-Attitude: Be the Difference

The Attitude for Success:
To keep Saboteurs from derailing your organization or team, you need to make sure they feel valued. Helping them feel valued starts with identifying any emotional baggage or past disappointments that are keeping them rooted in this behavior. Help them turn past setbacks into setups to become better. Showing them ways they can make a positive difference creates a win-win situation for everyone.

_____

_____

_____

_____

_____

_____

_____

Personal vendettas harm more than their intended victims.

List the action steps needed to remove the *"I"* from an *Aint Nobody Gonna Win* member of your team in order to help him or her move to the ranks of the A.N.T.S. (**A**ttitudes **N**avigating **T**oward **S**uccess):

_____

_____

_____

_____

_____

_____

Are you a Saboteur?
☐ Always ☐ Frequently ☐ Sometimes ☐ Seldom ☐ Never

Is yours a "can do" or a "can't do" attitude? Circle the words that immediately come to mind when a new project is proposed.

Bummer	Not again!	Not doable
No way!	Finally!	Yes
Silly	Stupid	No
Not today	Brilliant	Don't
Can't	Won't	Certainly
Bonanza	Can't	Impossible
Maybe	Shouldn't	Great
Possibilities	Unrealistic	When

Every path has a few puddles.

UNKNOWN

_____

_____

_____

_____

_____

_____

_____

_____

_____

_____

_____

_____

_____

_____

_____

_____

_____

_____

_____

In the middle of difficulty lies opportunity.

ALBERT EINSTEIN

Additional Aint Profiles

E arlier in the book, you read descriptions of four pesky aints—WIIFM (What's In It For Me), Pretender, Slacker, and Saboteur—whose attitudes and behaviors negatively impacted their colleagues and nearly ruined the organization. It would take several volumes to characterize the number of aints we encounter in our daily lives and workplaces. But, no doubt, you get the idea—for every aint there is a corresponding Guiding Principle Step (GPS) and Be-Attitude you can adopt to navigate through to success.

The previous profiles, like the three you're about to read, were designed to give you insight on how to move from the ranks of the aints to becoming one of the A.N.T.S. (**A**ttitudes **N**avigating **T**oward **S**uccess).

Through the following profiles and exercises, you'll get to know Free Agent, whose selfish ambition hurts everyone; Faultfinder, a critic who makes life miserable; and Change Resister, who fears the unknown and refuses to change regardless of the cost. Their stories appear in the original *What's Bugging You?* book.

Code Name: Free Agent
Aint on the Team

Free Agents often think, "I don't need anybody's help. I know what I'm doing. I don't need the team. The team needs me. Besides, you have to make your own way in the world and hope for the best. Who cares who gets hurt?"

They are people who do not choose to see the value of working with others. Free Agents often feel like they perform their jobs better than others on the team, which is why they feel compelled to question the qualifications and purpose of the team. They tend to make their own personal agenda the priority.

While many Free Agents are very talented, one of their top goals should be to make those around them better. The reason is obvious to everyone on Free Agent's team—when the team wins, everybody wins. *The key to success for Free Agents is collaboration and getting everyone to see the importance of the roles they play.* No one person is more valuable than the team.

The Guiding Principle Step (GPS):
Teamwork—Live the Vision
and the Be-Attitude: *Be Supportive*

Are you a Free Agent?
☐ Always ☐ Frequently ☐ Sometimes ☐ Seldom ☐ Never

Is your commitment to the good of the team? ☐ Yes ☐ No
Explain why you feel the way you do.

_____

_____

_____

_____

_____

_____

_____

_____

_____

_____

_____

Whom or what are you committed to? How do you demonstrate and express your commitment?

_____

_____

_____

_____

_____

_____

_____

_____

_____

_____

_____

_____

_____

_____

_____

_____

_____

_____

_____

_____

_____

_____

_____

_____

_____

_____

_____

_____

_____

_____

_____

_____

_____

_____

Individual commitment to a group effort—
that is what makes a team work, a company work,
a society work, a civilization work.

VINCE LOMBARDI

Take this self-assessment.

Does your attitude support the team?
☐ Always ☐ Frequently ☐ Sometimes ☐ Seldom ☐ Never

Do you apologize when you cause harm—whether intentional or not—to another person?
☐ Always ☐ Frequently ☐ Sometimes ☐ Seldom ☐ Never

Do you sincerely thank others for their kindnesses and generosity?
☐ Always ☐ Frequently ☐ Sometimes ☐ Seldom ☐ Never

Are you a giver?
☐ Always ☐ Frequently ☐ Sometimes ☐ Seldom ☐ Never

Are you a taker?
☐ Always ☐ Frequently ☐ Sometimes ☐ Seldom ☐ Never

Are you a pushover?
☐ Always ☐ Frequently ☐ Sometimes ☐ Seldom ☐ Never

Do you play the role of the martyr seeking sympathy or
attention for a real or imagined hurt or slight?
☐ Always ☐ Frequently ☐ Sometimes ☐ Seldom ☐ Never

Do you laugh when you're nervous or uncomfortable?
☐ Always ☐ Frequently ☐ Sometimes ☐ Seldom ☐ Never
   If so, is this behavior misunderstood?
☐ Always ☐ Frequently ☐ Sometimes ☐ Seldom ☐ Never

Does your teasing ever get out of control?
☐ Always ☐ Frequently ☐ Sometimes ☐ Seldom ☐ Never

Do you bail out of situations leaving others to clean up after you?
☐ Always ☐ Frequently ☐ Sometimes ☐ Seldom ☐ Never

Do you quit when things get tough?
☐ Always ☐ Frequently ☐ Sometimes ☐ Seldom ☐ Never

Do you complain when you can't figure things out?
☐ Always ☐ Frequently ☐ Sometimes ☐ Seldom ☐ Never

Do you blame others for your shortcomings?
☐ Always ☐ Frequently ☐ Sometimes ☐ Seldom ☐ Never

My business is not to remake myself,
but to make the absolute best of what God made.

ROBERT BROWNING

Based on your responses on the checklist items, do you consider yourself a team player? List ten characteristics team players exhibit.

1.
_____

_____

2.
_____

_____

3.
_____

_____

4.
_____

_____

5.
_____

_____

6.
_____

_____

7.
_____

_____

8.
_____

_____

9.
_____

_____

10.
_____

_____

Check all that apply:

I am:

☐ an attentive listener

☐ diligent

☐ willing to take on new tasks

☐ motivated

☐ dependable

☐ punctual

☐ an effective communicator

☐ understanding

☐ optimistic

☐ open minded

☐ helpful

☐ cynical

☐ truthful

☐ a self-starter

☐ trustworthy

☐ supportive

☐ willing to learn new skills

☐ a thoughtful colleague

☐ always prepared

☐ enthusiastic

☐ sincere

☐ slow to anger

☐ hopeful

☐ fair

☐ non-judgmental

☐ a realist

☐ tenacious

☐ respectful of all team members

---

*It is never too late
to be what you might have been.*

GEORGE ELIOT

Check all that apply:

I:

☐ don't gossip

☐ respect leadership

☐ volunteer my time and resources

☐ seek opportunities for personal/professional development

☐ seek ways to work more efficiently

☐ set high standards for myself

☐ expect the best

☐ seek solutions to problems

☐ encourage other team members

☐ accept responsibility for my actions

☐ mentor young team members

☐ judge people

☐ judge behavior, not people

☐ seek solutions to problems

☐ make constructive suggestions

_____

_____

_____

_____

_____

_____

_____

_____

_____

_____

_____

_____

_____

_____

_____

_____

_____

_____

_____

_____

_____

_____

_____

*The voice of our original self is often muffled,
overwhelmed, even strangled,
by the voices of other people's expectations.*

JULIA CAMERON

How do your actions support the team's agenda?

_____

_____

_____

_____

_____

_____

_____

_____

_____

_____

_____

_____

We cannot become what we need to be
by remaining what we are.

MAX DEPREE

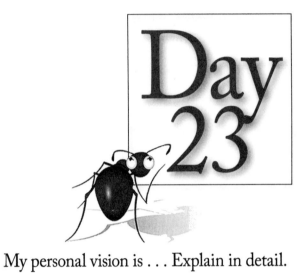

My personal vision is . . . Explain in detail.

_____

_____

_____

_____

_____

_____

_____

_____

_____

_____

_____

_____

My team's vision for me is . . . Explain in detail.

_____

_____

_____

_____

_____

_____

_____

_____

_____

_____

_____

_____

_____

_____

_____

_____

The future belongs to those who believe
in the beauty of their dreams.

ELEANOR ROOSEVELT

Code Name: Faultfinder
Aint to Blame

"It ain't my fault. I told you they didn't know what they were doing. I did my job. . . I blame this on management and the other departments. Someone else should take the blame for this mess," grumbles Faultfinder.

A Faultfinder is a person who criticizes and regularly finds reason to blame others and pick apart projects. They are finger-pointers who tend to make life miserable for others. In the long run, Faultfinders tend to run people away.

Faultfinders should focus on constructive solutions in order to make things better instead of concentrating on current or past problems. They should also remember that when they point one finger at someone else, there will always be three fingers pointing back at them. So, three to one, Faultfinders will find the solution within themselves. *The key to success for Faultfinders is accountability.*

The Guiding Principle Step (GPS):
Accountability—Say NO to the Blame Game
and the Be-Attitude: *Be Accountable*

Are you a Faultfinder?
☐ Always ☐ Frequently ☐ Sometimes ☐ Seldom ☐ Never

Faultfinders harbor resentment and are often bitter over past slights. What behaviors or attitudes might you expect from a Faultfinder?

Quick to anger

Holds a grudge

_____

_____

_____

_____

_____

_____

_____

_____

_____

_____

_____

_____

_____

_____

_____

_____

_____

_____

_____

_____

_____

_____

_____

_____

_____

_____

_____

_____

_____

_____

_____

_____

_____

_____

_____

_____

_____

I've learned that people will forget what you said,
people will forget what you did, but people will never forget
how you made them feel.

MAYA ANGELOU

Code Name: Change Resister
Aint Changing

"Why do we have to change it?" asks Change Resister. "If it's not broken, why don't we just leave it alone? None of these changes make sense to me . . . Things are sure not like they used to be."

Fear of the unknown is the main reason why people don't embrace change. Change Resisters regularly fight it, even when the familiar is unsatisfactory and counterproductive. Uncomfortable embracing new ideas, they procrastinate. Often dragging their feet when challenged to adopt new procedures, Change Resisters reject concepts, processes, and technology that change the way they have to do things.

The key to success for a Change Resister is recognizing that in change there is the power for growth. The only difference between a rut and a grave are the dimensions. To encourage Change Resisters, always communicate the benefits of the transition to help them stay focused on the positive aspects of moving forward.

The Guiding Principle Step (GPS):
Embrace Change—Convert Turning Points to Learning Points
and the Be-Attitude: *Be a Change Embracer*

Are you a Change Resister?
☐ Always ☐ Frequently ☐ Sometimes ☐ Seldom ☐ Never

As quickly as possible, without much deliberating, jot down some of your fears. Anything that crosses your mind, jot it down.

_____

_____

_____

_____

_____

_____

_____

_____

_____

_____

_____

_____

Reread your responses. Circle those items that are actually based on reality. Cross out those fears that are merely in your head. For each item you circled, list positive steps you can take to reduce your level of fear.

_____

_____

_____

_____

_____

_____

_____

_____

_____

_____

_____

_____

_____

_____

_____

_____

_____

What things in your life do you have the power to change?

_____

_____

_____

_____

_____

_____

_____

_____

_____

_____

_____

_____

_____

_____

_____

_____

_____

_____

Embrace change with a no-fear attitude.

How do you respond to fear? Do you act or react?

_____

_____

_____

_____

_____

_____

_____

_____

_____

_____

Life shrinks or expands in proportion to one's courage.

ANAIS NIN

People often shy away from change because they fear the unknown, or don't want to take the time to learn new concepts or explore new territory. List the areas in your life that you'd most like to change.

_____

_____

_____

_____

_____

_____

_____

_____

_____

_____

How do you typically respond to change? Embrace it with a winning attitude? Resist it kicking and screaming?

_____

_____

_____

_____

_____

_____

_____

_____

When was the last time you initiated change (at home, on the team, at work, or at school)?

_____

_____

_____

_____

_____

_____

_____

_____

Did you achieve your desired outcome? Explain in detail.

_____

_____

_____

_____

_____

_____

_____

_____

_____

_____

_____

_____

_____

_____

_____

_____

_____

_____

_Nothing is so perfectly amusing as
a total change of ideas._

LAURENCE STERN

What things in your life do you have the power to change?

_____

_____

_____

_____

_____

_____

_____

_____

_____

_____

_____

_____

_____

_____

_____

_____

_____

_____

_____

_____

What are the benefits of making these changes to you, your team, and your organization?

_____

_____

_____

_____

_____

_____

_____

_____

_____

_____

_____

The choice to change is yours.

    The beginning of wisdom is to call things by their right names. Naming gives power to our words, intentions, and actions. When you name a behavior, it becomes real to you. And it is only then that you can begin to change it.

Name your bad behaviors:

1. _____

2. _____

3. _____

4. _____

5. _____

6. _____

7. _____

8. _____

9. _____

10. _____

For each of the bad behaviors previously listed, *name one simple thing* you can do within the next seven days to start breaking that habit.

1. _____

2. _____

3. _____

4. _____

5. _____

6. _____

7. _____

8. _____

9. _____

10. _____

Actions speak louder than words
but not nearly as often.

MARK TWAIN

Our Friends the Ants

They live in colonies. They are a diverse community. Resilient and self-sacrificing team members, they are highly intuitive. Conscientious workers, they are extremely resourceful and creative in their solutions. They are great mentors. And they accomplish impossible feats for their size.

List three ANT behaviors that you model.

1. _____

_____

2. _____

_____

3. _____

_____

List three AINT behaviors that may have impacted your
attitude and behavior.

1. _____

_____

2. _____

_____

3. _____

_____

Are there any AINTS on your team or in your organization?
If yes, name them:

_____

_____

_____

_____

_____

_____

_____

_____

_____

Which AINT best describes you?

☐ Aint on the Team
☐ Aint to Blame
☐ Aint Doing That Job
☐ Aint Trying
☐ Aint Ethical
☐ Aint Changing
☐ Aint Nobody Gonna Win

_____

_____

(Name your own AINT behavior)

How does this AINT attitude affect your relationship with others?

_____

_____

_____

_____

_____

_____

_____

_____

_____

We can do no great things, only small things with great love.

MOTHER TERESA

Better or Bitter?

Adopting a negative attitude when your work goes unrecognized, or when you are slighted, betrayed or disrespected, puts you in jeopardy of becoming bitter, particularly if you're unwilling to accept an apology and forgive the offending party.

Forgiveness allows you to make peace with yourself. Letting go of anger, disappointment, and frustration, when faced with opposition or indifference, will allow you to maintain your integrity and standards. Never underestimate the power of your attitude and your words. Resorting to toxic talk or spreading gossip will only make the situation worse.

Gossip, the "derogatory critique," erodes trust and morale, and serves no useful purpose. Individuals who frequently engage in gossip do so, either consciously or unconsciously, to lower the esteem of another in an effort to raise their own self worth. Envy, back biting, hostility, criticism, sarcasm—all forms of invalidation—are, like gossip, injurious and destructive, whether directed at others or oneself.

Remember, no deed—positive or negative—goes unnoticed. So, guard your ear gate, monitor your eye gate, control your mouth gate, and before you realize it you will have gained a reputation for taking the higher ground.

Bitter or better? How do you handle disappointment?

_____

_____

_____

_____

_____

_____

_____

_____

_____

_____

Emotions are not "good" or "bad," although how we act on our emotions is not always wise or justified. Expressing emotion is healthy as long as you're not judging, blaming, berating, or doing harm to others or yourself in the process. When faced with disappointment, feel the emotion and deal with the situation as soon as possible. Use it as an opportunity to find the lesson in the challenge.

_____

_____

_____

_____

_____

_____

_____

_____

_____

_____

_____

_____

_____

_____

_____

_____

_____

_____

_____

We all need a daily checkup from the neck up.

ZIG ZIGLAR

What are your three greatest strengths? List them.

1. _____

2. _____

3. _____

Circle the adjectives that best describe you:

Reliable	Intelligent	Witty
Boisterous	Helpful	Stubborn
Generous	Ambitious	Professional
Boastful	Competent	Truthful
Passionate	Sweet	Calculating
Pessimistic	Lazy	Mean
Energetic	Average	Judgmental
Gracious	Moral	Super-fantastic
Flexible	Angry	Spontaneous
Leader	Follower	Loner

Engaging	Responsive	Calm
Cautious	Belligerent	Talented
Creative	Engaging	Shy
Slow	Talkative	Unprepared
Courteous	Kind	Compassionate

Write a description of how you view yourself.

_____

_____

_____

_____

_____

_____

_____

_____

_____

_____

_____

_____

_____

_____

_____

_____

_____

Write a description of how your closest friend would describe you.

_____

_____

_____

_____

_____

_____

_____

_____

_____

_____

_____

_____

_____

_____

_____

_____

_____

_____

_____

_____

_____

_____

_____

_____

_____

_____

_____

_____

_____

_____

_____

_____

_____

_____

_____

_____

_____

To love oneself is the beginning of a life-long romance.

OSCAR WILDE

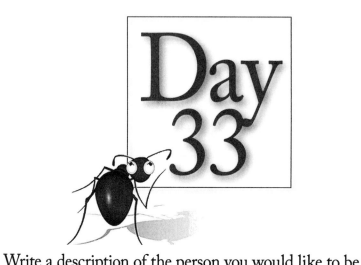

Write a description of the person you would like to be.

_____

_____

_____

_____

_____

_____

_____

_____

_____

_____

_____

_____

_____

_We must not allow other people's limited perceptions
to define us._

VIRGINIA SATIR

The state of our relationships has a direct impact on our over-all well-being. Take time to fully explore how your relationships are affecting your success.

Name your allies:

_____

_____

_____

_____

_____

List the toxic people you spend too much time with:

_____

_____

_____

_____

How have your relationships impacted your ability to achieve
your personal goals? To support the team?

_____

_____

_____

_____

_____

_____

_____

_____

_____

_____

_____

_____

_____

_____

Little kindnesses and courtesies are so important.
In relationships, the little things are the big things.

STEPHEN R. COVEY

List three people you can depend on:

1. _____

2. _____

3. _____

List three people who can depend on you:

1. _____

2. _____

3. _____

Do you generally go out of your way to help others?
Yes ☐ No ☐

If so, how? If not, why?

_____

_____

Ability without dependability has no value.

UNKNOWN

Do you plan ahead? Or do you procrastinate and hope for the best? How does this behavior impact your success? Affect your attitude?

_____

_____

_____

_____

_____

_____

_____

_____

_____

_____

Everything can be taken from a man but one thing:
the last of the human freedoms—to choose one's attitude
in any given set of circumstances, to choose one's own way.

VIKTOR E. FRANKL

Each one of us is a work-in-progress, hopefully growing more wise and mature with the opportunities and challenges that life brings. While your outlook may change depending on external factors, the core of your being is shaped by your beliefs and values: what you feel, think, judge, honor, love, hate, desire, hope for, and esteem.

Many of our core beliefs and values were passed on to us by our parents and caregivers. We are dynamic, spiritual beings, forever changing as we grow. What values and beliefs are you holding onto that might be hindering your attitude?

I can't get any better.

I'm too old.

I'll never get ahead.

_____

_____

_____

_____

_____

_____

_____

_____

_____

_____

_____

_____

_____

_____

_____

_____

_____

_____

Belief creates the actual fact.

WILLIAM JAMES

How can you put your attitude into action? As quickly as possible, list all the ways you can think of. (*Example*: I can be an attentive listener.)

_____

_____

_____

_____

_____

_____

_____

_____

_____

_____

_____

_____

_____

_____

_____

_____

_____

_____

_____

_____

_____

_____

_____

_____

_____

_____

_____

Your programming creates your belief,
your belief creates your attitude.

How has your positive or negative attitude affected your success?

_____

_____

_____

_____

_____

_____

_____

_____

_____

_____

_____

_____

_____

_____

_____

_____

_____

How has your positive or negative attitude affected your relationships?

_____

_____

_____

_____

_____

_____

_____

_____

_____

_____

_____

_____

_____

_____

Guard your heart, it's the control center
for your attitude.

Awards and Rewards—
In the Winners Circle

You've just received the Award for Best_____.
Choose an activity or skill you would like to be recognized for
or one that you plan to accomplish. This is the time to envision
yourself having completed a desired goal or dream. Visualization
is a powerful tool for achieving goals, and for making changes
in attitude and behavior. Write why you are deserving of this
award.

_____

_____

_____

_____

_____

_____

_____

_____

_____

_____

_____

_____

_____

_____

_____

_____

_____

_____

_____

_____

_____

_____

I hated every minute of training, but I said, "Don't quit. Suffer now and live the rest of your life as a champion."

MUHAMMAD ALI

Write your acceptance speech. Whom would you thank?
How did the team assist you in winning?

_____

_____

_____

_____

_____

_____

_____

_____

_____

_____

_____

_____

_____

_____

_____

Stand in front of the mirror. Look yourself in the eyes. In a
clear, strong voice read your acceptance speech. Thank all the
people who made this award possible. Give yourself a pat on the
back and bask in your victory.

You've been named Employee/Teammate of the Year. Were you awarded for being a team leader? Taking initiative? Solving a problem? Innovative thinking? A thoughtful gesture? Write a page explaining your accomplishment. Use additional paper, if needed.

_____

_____

_____

_____

_____

_____

_____

Refer back to your Award for Best_____ and Employee/Teammate of the Year as often as needed.

Stand in front of the mirror and reread your speeches or read them to a *trusted* and *supportive* friend or team member, who will respond favorably. In an earlier exercise (Day 34), you named your allies. Naming gives power to our words, intentions, and actions.

Make the most of yourself, for that is all there is of you.

RALPH WALDO EMERSON

Only you can change you. Now is the time to make the change you've been seeking. *It's time to fire your problems.* As your own boss, write yourself a memo and put your problems on notice. Tell them "You're fired!" This is not a time to beat yourself up. This is a time for an objective assessment of your bad behaviors and "stinking thinking." Put pen to paper and write that overdue termination notice.

Problems, you've been hanging around here too long. It's time to go! You're fired . . .

Dream to be more than you are.

Stand in front of a mirror. Look yourself in the eyes and forcefully read your problems their termination notice. For the next seven days, repeat this exercise. On the seventh day, put an x through the memo as a reminder that your problems no longer have the same hold over you.

_____

_____

_____

_____

_____

_____

_____

_____

Go to Day 2 and retake the Rate Your Attitude exercise to determine how your attitude has changed in the past 38 days.

Reread your signed Contract on page 7 and enter today's date on the second blank line. Now take a moment to reflect on the changes in your attitude, noting the difference in those things that once bugged you and your team.

A true commitment is a heartfelt promise to yourself from which you will not back down.

DAVID MCNALLY

The Optimist Creed
Read daily.

Promise yourself . . .

- To be so strong that nothing can disturb your peace of mind.

- To talk health, happiness, and prosperity to every person you meet.

- To make all your friends feel that there is something special in them.

- To look at the sunny side of everything and make your optimism come true.

- To think only of the best, to work only for the best, and to expect only the best.

- To be just as enthusiastic about the success of others as you are about your own.

- To forget the mistakes of the past and press on to the greater achievements of the future.

- To wear a cheerful countenance at all times and give every living creature you meet a smile.

- To give so much time to the improvement of yourself that you have no time to criticize others.

- To be too large for worry, too noble for anger, too strong for fear, and too happy to permit the presence of trouble.

The Seven Guiding Principle Steps (GPS) and Be-Attitudes

Clip and save this reminder of the seven **Guiding Principle Steps (GPS)** and **Be-Attitudes** that will help you navigate through and around everyday challenges and to develop a *super-fantastic attitude*.

Teamwork— Live the Vision	Be Supportive
Accountability— Say No to the Blame Game	Be Accountable
Ethical Execution— Do What's Right Because It's Right	Be Performance- and Integrity-Driven
Embrace Change— Convert Turning Points to Learning Points	Be a Change Embracer
Commit to Win— Do More Than is Expected	Be Coachable
Awareness — Notice What's Needed and Do What's Necessary	Be Responsible
Attitude is Everything— If Something Is Wrong, Make It Right	Be the Difference

Congratulations on completing this workbook and journal! If this process has been helpful to you, we would love to hear your story of how this book has helped motivate a change in your attitude. Email us at info@superfantastic.com.

For your free attitude self-assessment, or to order your copy of the *What's Bugging You?* book, go to www.superfantastic.com.